Fish Tales and Other Stories …

Fish Tales and Other Stories ...

as told by
Capt. Gus Gustafson

iUniverse, Inc.
New York Lincoln Shanghai

Fish Tales and Other Stories ...

iUniverse books may be ordered through booksellers or by contacting:

iUniverse
2021 Pine Lake Road, Suite 100
Lincoln, NE 68512
www.iuniverse.com
1-800-Authors (1-800-288-4677)

ISBN: 978-0-595-43348-3 (pbk)
ISBN: 978-0-595-87674-7 (ebk)

Printed in the United States of America

Contents

Introduction

Readers beware! These stories, as sincere and honest as they might appear, are fabrications of an idle mind. Each story is told as if it actually happened. Don't believe them, but please enjoy reading them!

This book is the first in a series of short stories that feature my favorite fishing tales. I grew up listening to stories told by my father and a group of charter boat fishing captains. My dad was a master of the tall tale and my mom spent hours reading stories to the three sons. I later passed on this family tradition to my son, Toby. Today, I write a monthly fish tale for a page on my web site, FishingWith-Gus.com, and I continue to tell stories to anyone who will listen.

Throughout this book you will find names like Rawhide, Catawba Cat, Deere Jon and Fishmore. These fictional characters are composites of actual personalities that Capt. Gus has shared experiences with over the years. Each story has some basis for truth, but over time has become better described as a fish tale.

Rawhide is a crusty old striper fisherman obsessed with catching trophy fish and winning tournaments. Things don't always go well for this proud angler, but he keeps trying.

Catawba Cat will tell a lie at the drop of a hat. He even begins to believe his own lies. Hundred pound catfish, thirty-five pound mullet and a close encounter with an African Elephant in South Carolina are all merely a way of life for this catfish guide.

Deere Jon, Catawba's brother, fishes for thousand pound sturgeon at Santee Cooper, while Fishmore attempts to open a theme park for bass fishermen.

If you like dog stories, you'll love the one about a fishing dog that was banned from bass tournaments.

There is also the story about Splash, a big striped bass that tangles with a submarine, and one about Lobo, a mussel eating river creature.

These bigger than life stories go from land sharks and earthquakes to gold mines filled with largemouth bass.

I hope you will enjoy reading this book as much as I enjoyed writing it.

Special thanks to Susan Gustafson, Anne Silver, and Amy Myers for their encouragement and assistance with the editing and to Matt Myers of Bedford Falls Graphics for his illustrations and layout of "Fish Tales and Other Stories as told by Capt. Gus."

Wag, the Fishing Dog

The best fishing partner I ever had was a dog, named Wag. Wag was a mixed breed the color of a golden Labrador retriever, but much smaller. Behind his ears were small gill slits just behind the cheekbones on both sides of his head. His most amazing features were his webbed hind feet. They were probably the reason he was not allowed to participate in any TV dog paddling shows.

Wag was a kind hearted and honest fishing dog. We spent hours together on many lakes in North and South Carolina. He stood sentry on the bow, while I maneuvered down the bank with an electric trolling motor on the stern. Wag pointed when a fish swirled, or if he sensed that one might be under a fallen log or beneath a dock. When a fish was hooked, Wag's bark was like a cheer. The more the fish jumped, the faster his tail would wag, thus his name. When a fish was successfully landed and unhooked, Wag lightly touched it with his nose, an indication to me that he wanted it returned to the water. In addition to being honest, he was a staunch believer in catch and release.

Wag performed best when fishing was slow. He became frustrated if I didn't catch a fish within an hour or so. At times he would sniff the lid of my tackle box, a sign to me that I was using the wrong lure. I would open the box and Wag used his right front paw to point to a lure that was sure to catch a fish on the next cast. Next he would do his "fish dog thing" by scratching the slits behind his cheekbones with his webbed hind feet. Once this ritual was completed, he would dive under water and search for fish. When he located a school, he returned to the surface, jumped back in the boat and pointed in the general direction of the fish he had found. More times than not, I would hook a fish on the next cast, while his tail wagged profusely.

We fished together for a long time; we even fished some tournaments. After winning ten or twelve in a row, other anglers got suspicious. When they realized that Wag was finding the fish and choosing the proper lures to use, we were banned from the tournament trail.

As time passed, Wag couldn't swim as fast or as deeply as he once did. He finally retired and spent his last years at a summer camp for homeless boys. Each time the kids came to fish, he was there to patrol the edge of the pond and point to nesting bream in the shallows.

Be reminded that small fish have … *LARGE TALES!*

Wobbly

In the early 1990's, the dam of a small pond broke and the fish population escaped. The pond was managed by a group of biologists experimenting with the cross breeding of Arkansas Blue Catfish and Wyoming Buffalo Carp. Their goal was to create a fish that would grow quickly and make tasty table fare.

One free-swimming fish found its way into a 32,000-acre impoundment located in the Piedmont region of North Carolina. As soon as the fish discovered open water, it headed upstream and swam for twenty miles. The spillway of a dam that fed the lake from up river halted its northerly progress. It was in these clear, cool tailrace waters filled with forage fish that it took up residence.

In its new environment, the fish quickly grew to gigantic proportions. Year after year it lazily swam undetected in the deep water below the dam. By the fourth year, its appearance became somewhat eerie. At first glance, it resembled an oversized channel bass, but a second look revealed a shark-like appearance. Regardless of what one thought, the mind's eye saw a fish larger than "Jaws." It was now too large to hide, and rumors of a local sea monster spread quickly.

The fish became known as "Wobbly" because it wobbled when it swam. The wobbly action was probably due to a missing fin that some believe was broken when the big fish became lodged between the pilings of a railroad bridge. Rumor has it that after quite a struggle, it lost the fin while trying to free itself from the bridge.

Anglers came from as far away as Mississippi to try their skills at catching Wobbly. To lure the fish, one angler actually gang-hooked a goat to a rope, tied the free end to the bumper of his pickup truck, and set the poor goat afloat. Wobbly couldn't resist a goat swimming on the surface. He quickly swallowed it, and pulled the truck into the water as he swam away. When the rope finally parted, Wobbly swam toward the railroad bridge just as a train was passing over the trestle.

The old structure shook from the force of the southbound fish, and the passenger train swayed violently from side to side. The erratic motion of the train caused the bridge pilings to buckle just enough to allow Wobbly to squeeze through the opening. As he cleared the bridge, the train and all of the passengers went tumbling into the water below.

Rescue workers were on the scene within minutes. Helicopters, fireboats and lake patrol vessels quickly appeared to save the passengers. Most had scrapes and bruises, but none were seriously injured.

Following the incident, the investigation concluded that Wobbly was the cause of the derailment. Afterwards, he was nowhere to be found. Some believe that he made his way back to the lower end of the lake where he now lives somewhere in very deep water.

Recently, a state record catfish of more than eighty pounds was taken from the lake. Those who saw it thought it looked somewhat like an Arkansas Blue Catfish, while others thought it resembled a Wyoming Buffalo Carp. Could it have been Wobbly's first born?

Be reminded that small fish have … *LARGE TALES!*

North Myrtle Beach

Fairy tales begin with "once upon a time," while fish stories are often prefaced by, "this is no lie." What you are about to read is not a fairy tale. The events of this September morning will be fodder for fish stories for years to come.

It began as an end of summer trip to the beach for a group of Denver, NC residents. While the ladies were out shopping, Mike Bradshaw, James Summerlin, and Pete Williams decided to spend the day fishing in the surf of North Myrtle Beach.

It was low tide when they left Mike's oceanfront condo on foot, with Mike leading the way. He was dressed like a real south Florida "get-a-guide" in his long billed cap, sunglasses and matching nylon shirt and shorts with numerous flap-covered pockets.

Mike began the day by scanning the horizon for what he considered the perfect stretch of beach to surf fish. His definition of perfect was where the ocean currents bring the biggest fish within eating distance of a helpless shrimp on a rusty hook. In his left hand he carried a blue plastic bag from Wal-Mart that served as a tackle box. In his right hand he had three fishing rods and a pair of sand spikes to cradle the rods.

James followed shortly behind with the beach chairs and a large paper bag filled with snacks. Pete had an ice chest full of drinks and a five-gallon bucket of dirty water that contained a dozen dying shrimp. The shrimp were purchased earlier by Lindy Sikes, who had remained at the condo to nurse his third degree sunburned body.

James and Pete began to tire from the long trek up the beach. Pete was beginning to question the self-appointed guide's fishing prowess, and was thinking that he most likely would refuse to walk much farther. At this low moment in time, the morning silence was broken by a shrill yell from Mike. "This is the spot!" he shouted. "This is the spot!" The other two looked around, but saw absolutely nothing different at all about this particular spot. The sand and sea were exactly the same as they had been for the past hour they had walked and carried their gear. Pete questioned Mike's reasoning on why they hadn't driven to the spot to begin with. Mike didn't respond.

Finally, at this "perfect spot," the fishing trip was officially underway. James unfolded the beach chairs, Pete baited a hook with a dead shrimp, and Mike set the two sand spikes near the water's edge. James questioned why there were only two spikes when they had three rods. Mike claimed that a big fish had pulled the other spike, along with the rod, into the deep blue water at this exact spot a year ago. Perhaps this was the real answer as to why they stopped here and hopefully a good omen for a perfect day of fishing.

The anglers settled into their beach chairs and occasionally glanced at the lines. The butt of the third rod, the one without the spike, was stuck in the sand. The weary trio dozed as the tide began to creep in. Pete was the first to awaken. The rising tide had surrounded his chair and the seawater had soaked his bottom.

Minutes later, the drag on Mike's reel began to sing, as a big fish quickly pulled the line. Mike jumped to reach for the rod, but not in time. The fish had yanked the butt of the rod from the sand and was towing it out to sea. Mike chased after it and was able to grab it, just as a large breaker crested and soaked him from head to toe. In the midst of this episode, James awakened in time to witness the drenching, and noticed that Mike's rod was doubled over. Pete and James began to yell encouragements as the huge fish jumped.

The battle raged for quite some time. The fish had taken most of the line, then changed directions and decided to swim to shore. Mike's challenge now was to keep the slack from the line, and this he could not do with the fast swimming fish coming so quickly in his direction. The faster he reeled, the faster the fish swam. In order to keep the line taut, James yelled to Mike to run backwards up the sand. Mike backpedaled until he found himself half way to North Ocean Drive Boulevard. It was there that he tripped and fell backwards over two beach chairs and an oversized umbrella. All the while, James was shouting, "Keep the line tight!"

The frantic owner of the umbrella and chairs came running down the beach to get a closer look at what was happening. Her beach gear was fine, but Mike's wet body was covered with sand and his left leg was bleeding profusely from the collision. He was a mess, but the fish was still hooked and floundering in the surf.

As Pete and James headed to the water, they could not believe how big it really was—much larger than they had thought. James tried to grab it by the mouth as it swam by, but the fish swam through his legs and knocked him down. Pete finally pounced on the big fish and held it until James could help him pull it to the beach.

Mike was so overwhelmed when he realized the big fish had been captured, that he began to jump up and down and hug the "beach chair lady!" James tried to cram the fish in the shrimp bucket, but it was much too large and it flopped out and about on the sand.

In all the excitement, no one thought to take a picture of the prize until long after they had released it. They were so excited that they even let it go before they knew what it was. Pete thought it was a Marlin, James, a Channel Bass. No one knew for sure, not even Mike.

When they returned to Denver, they found a tarpon mount that belonged to Craig Price. Mike thought it closely resembled his fish. Another friend, Ron Poe, took the picture of Mike with the mounted fish. Mike said the picture was taken for posterity, whatever that means.

Be reminded that small fish have … *LARGE TALES!*

Lobo

Generations of Kat family members made their living fishing, trapping and trading on the river. The legendary Grand Kat, as he was affectionately known, was the great-great grandfather of Little Kat. Grand Kat was the best trader around. He bartered for anything, including furs, catfish, lumber and even bird feathers. In return, he supplied the natives with guns, dynamite and jugs of firewater. Over time, settlers filled the river valley and forced the natives to find solace elsewhere. The Kat family remained and continued to derive their livelihood from the river.

Kat Kat, Little Kat's famous grandfather, plied the river daily in search of catfish and river mussels. The river catfish were so tasty that they were once served on the Queen of England's dining table. The only morsels more tasty were the sweet river mussels that the catfish fed upon. The demand for river cats was so great, that eventually there were no more to be caught.

When that happened, Big Kat, Little Kat's dad, invented a special rake that allowed the mussels to be harvested without cracking their paper-thin shells. The Kat family, who gathered and shipped mussels to markets near and far, made a small fortune. When Big Kat reached seventy years of age, he relinquished his business to Little Kat and the family venture continued to prosper.

Legend has it that a creature of great size named Lobo, appeared from time to time and terrorized the citizens of the river community. The mere mention of his name struck fear in the hearts of everyone.

It was early one fall when a mussel raker failed to return from the river bog at day's end. The investigation that followed produced one shredded white boot belonging to the victim. Shortly thereafter, a second, and then a third raker disappeared without a trace. The remaining mussel rakers quit. Little Kat was left to rake alone, while his wife Kitty Kat, shipped the sweet river mussels to the markets.

One morning, Little Kat was raking when he noticed a large wake headed in his direction. The wake was that of Lobo. The saber-toothed creature was just about to grab one of Little Kat's legs, but he was able to quickly jump aside. In the past, nets, hooks, lines and even explosives had not been able to deter Lobo, but Little Kat used the only weapon he had and began to beat Lobo with his rake. After quite a struggle, the creature finally disappeared into deep water. Afterwards, Little Kat pondered for days before designing a plan to rid the river of the toothy creature once and for all.

The next morning, the river was filled with workers wielding rakes and digging mussels. Each bushel of harvested mussels was taken to the bog south of town. By day's end, hundreds of bushels where stacked on the shore. Throughout the night, the mussels were broken and tossed into the water. Morning found the air filled with the staunch smell of mussels, and the river stained with the meat and juices from thousands of mollusks.

Lobo couldn't resist the temptation. He spent the best part of the week eating mussels, as each night a fresh supply was tossed into the bog. By Saturday, Lobo's stomach was so bloated that he could no longer swim. That night, Little Kat and his band of rakers returned to the bog to end the saga.

Months passed and nobody heard or mentioned a word about the departed monster. Then one day, a letter written on the Queen of England's stationary, was posted on the bulletin board at the town square. The royal chef was requesting that Kitty Kat ship another "sweet river creature" to the Queen's kitchen at Buckingham Palace.

Be reminded that small fish have … *LARGE TALES!*

Catawba Cat

The man holding court in the River City Tackle Shop was telling his tale to all who would listen. He stood between the spinner and crank bait sections where a small crowd was spellbound by his yarn.

The storyteller was dressed from head to toe in camouflaged clothing, but the patterns didn't match. His hat was two sizes too large, which allowed the bill to partially cover both eyes. The faded pants he wore were tattered and torn. His almost new shirt was wrinkled and covered with gobs of stuff. River mud caked the soles of his boots and the boot tops glistened with silver fish scales.

It took a few minutes for me to put it all together, but I finally surmised that the camouflaged man was either a commercial fisherman or a paid for hire get-a-guide. Nudging the fellow standing next to me, I asked, "Who is the dude spinning his yarn?" I was told to hush up and listen, so listen I did. The man was a river guide who specialized in fishing for world record catfish. His handle was "Catawba," short for "Catawba Cat," his real nickname. The tale he expounded upon was about a morning fishing safari with a world famous outdoor writer.

It seems that the writer was doing a story about fishing for hundred pound plus catfish, and Catawba had offered to show him how to catch them. The trip began with a cool ride upstream in a twenty-two foot flat-bottom boat. They stopped at a log jam on a sharp turn in the river and secured the boat with a brush hook attached to a small line.

While the writer was taking pictures, Catawba lowered a king size blue-black herring to the bottom. His heavy saltwater tackle consisted of a six-foot stand up tuna rod affixed to a 10/0 Penn International reel loaded with eighty-pound test monofilament line. The drag on the big gold reel was wrenched as tight as it could be to prevent a fish from pulling off any line. A twelve-ounce sinker and an 8/0 hook completed the rig.

Catawba told the writer that a big catfish had to be reeled to the surface in less than two minutes. Any time longer than that, the fish would realize it was hooked and would become tangled. He went on to say, that while fighting a big cat, one of three things was likely to happen. First, the tackle could break from the strain of the fight. Next, by having the drag so tightly set, the fish could pull the angler out of the boat. And finally, the fish could make it to the surface, be manhandled into the boat and bring about another challenge, since a one hundred pound catfish can wreck havoc with everything on deck. Catawba raised his pants leg and showed the writer where a big cat once stuck a fin through the muscle in the calf of his leg.

It wasn't long before Catawba set the hook on a big one and the boat began to rock. He wound down on the reel as hard as he could, and within a minute the fish was laying quietly on top of the water. Catawba's voice began to tremble and his face turned grim as he related the remainder of the story to his tackle shop audience. He said, "I knew I had a world record cat when I saw the head of the big fish amid ship and the tail out past the engine and wrapped around the stern." Quick math told him that the fish was at least fifteen feet long and over two hundred pounds.

Catawba yelled to the writer to get the gaff and stab the monster cat, but the writer didn't move. His fallen jaw was evidence that he was in awe with the size of the fish. Catawba barked his order several more times, but the writer was frozen in place. Finally, the fish realized he was hooked, shook his head a time or two and headed south toward "Davy Jones' Locker." The tuna rod broke from the surge, and the big cat swam away to fight another day.

Catawba ended his saga by blaming the writer for getting "Buck Fever" and costing him a world record. He vowed never to fish with the man again.

Be reminded that small fish have ... *LARGE TALES!*

Rawhide

A quick look at history tells us that Hide family members have been striper fishermen since colonial times. Striped bass, not turkey as legend has it, was served to the Pilgrims. Stripers at the first Thanksgiving dinner were caught by a man named Hide, who was among the first to set foot on Plymouth Rock. This settler/fisherman was a tough dude. He soon became known as "Raw Hide."

As time passed, the colonists became engaged in a War of Independence. General George Washington led the fight against the "Redcoats," and at his side was a member of the Hide family. The Revolutionary War hero known as "Col. Raw Hide," caught the stripers that fed the troops on that cold winter night before crossing the Delaware.

Stories of roaming buffalo herds lured another Hide member to the prairie. Single names were common west of the Mississippi, so eventually the family name was changed to Rawhide. This particular Rawhide, a young buffalo hunter, killed more Bison than all other hunters combined. He became a western legend. The old Rawhide TV shows tell of his sagas. Each time he crossed a river, he stopped his horse to cast a hook in hopes of catching a striper, but all he ever landed were sturgeons and trout. Eventually, he moved back east to striper fish in the Atlantic Ocean and to raise a family.

Later, a clan member known as Capt. Rawhide, piloted the freighter that sank many years ago near the location of today's Golden Gate Bridge. Its hull was filled with live striped bass in transit to a San Francisco Bay aquarium. The fish that escaped are believed to be ancestors of the stripers now swimming in the Pacific Ocean.

In the 1960's a lake was formed in the middle of the two Carolinas. Another man named Rawhide came on the scene. An exterminator by trade, he worked when necessary and fished the new lake when he wasn't killing spiders, bugs and ants.

A tiny insect began to invade the hulls of fiberglass boats by boring small holes in the surface. The insect was almost invisible, but it became a nuisance to the owners of every vessel moored on the big lake. It left a cavity in the fiberglass, similar to the wood damage caused by a termite. The fiberglass-eating machine was credited with the sinking of thousands of vessels. Entomologists were in a quandary, when Rawhide stepped up to the dock with a solution. Boaters were thrilled, and Rawhide acquired enough wealth to retire and fish all the time.

Early one morning, he came upon a spring that bubbled with millions of gallons of cool, oxygenated water. In these waters, swam hundreds of large, healthy striped bass. Rawhide had finally found the "happy fishing grounds" his ancestors had dreamed about. He knew this spot had to be kept a deep, dark secret. The mere mention of such a place would bring an onslaught of trophy hunters from near and far. Rawhide fished the spot on rare occasions, but only under the cover of fog or darkness. In his mind, the magical place was thought of as M-11.

During the next twenty years, he took a fish or two from the "honey hole" to win an occasional tournament. The legend of Rawhide grew with each big fish he brought to the tourney scales. Soon his reputation was larger than life. Pictures with his catches hang on the walls in many of the lake's seafood restaurants and tackle shops today.

Rawhide gained an unwelcome following that included a flotilla of boats filled with anglers who fished in his wake. At times, the number of vessels that trailed his planer boards formed what appeared to be a boat parade. A famous racecar driver gave him a concave rearview mirror that allowed him to watch his followers. If they were near, Rawhide stayed clear of the cherished lunker hole. To further protect his secret, he fished alone most of the time.

A few years ago, the largest striped bass tournament ever held was scheduled on Rawhide's lake. He fretted that the world's best anglers would uncover his secret, so he didn't venture near his "honey hole" during the entire pre-tournament fishing period. As luck would have it, the lake was covered by a thick fog bank the morning of the tournament. Rawhide slid into his secret place, attached a large crappie to his line, and quickly landed the biggest striper of his life. He estimated the fish to be more than sixty pounds. It was too large for his live well, so he partially filled the hull with lake water and allowed it to swim the length of the boat. He left his secret spot and fished for crappie near the weigh-in site for the rest of the day.

At the weigh-in, the big fish of the day was twenty-five pounds. Rawhide was the last to weigh his catch. The crowd roared and applauded as he toted the monster to the scales. The striper topped the scales at over eighty pounds, the largest ever taken from any freshwater impoundment.

As Rawhide crossed the stage to receive his rightful recognition, he tripped, and down he went. Three days later, he regained consciousness in a hospital bed. The concussion had erased all memory of his secret fishing hole. When he tries to recall its exact location, all he remembers is M-11, a green navigational marker.

Be reminded that small fish have … *LARGE TALES!*

Splash

The first time the gigantic striper was seen frolicking with a pod of bottle-nosed dolphins, it was cruising the beach in a deep trough between the second and third sand bars. The wading surf fishermen had never seen a striper of such enormous proportions. So taken aback were they, that none of them ventured a cast toward the monstrous linesider. They nervously watched in awe as it swam and played with the dolphins. Within seconds, the show was over. The cresting breakers had erased all signs of the striped bass and its bottle-nosed companions.

Following the sighting, the Big Surf Tackle Shop was abuzz with rumor and excitement. Each angler had a different take on what he or she had witnessed. One account proclaimed that the striper was larger than any whale, including Moby Dick, that ever swam in any of the Seven Seas. Another estimated the distance between the black stripes on the fish to be at least two feet. One old timer wasn't sure what he had seen, but he was positive that the "big one" would never be taken on a rod and reel.

The next morning found the beach elbow-to-elbow with surf casters. The weapons aimed toward the ocean and the rising sun were heavy-duty rods, not the buggy whip-like fresh water sticks or other ultra-light tackle. Disappointingly, there were now no signs of dolphin pods or super sized stripers. However, the whereabouts were soon discovered when a Mayday broadcast was heard blaring from the VHF radio in a nearby jeep.

It seemed that an angler fishing from a fifty-two-foot charter boat, had hooked a striper. After a prolonged battle, the big fish was brought close enough to be stabbed with a flying gaff. The fish jumped sky-high and landed squarely on the transom. Upon impact, the splintered vessel immediately began to take on seawater. The striper thumped free and made its way back into the ocean.

Soon there were reports on the ship-to-shore frequency that two boats were fighting the same huge fish. The super striper, now known as "Splash," had attacked the bait from yet another charter boat. A fierce battle raged as it took the line and headed in the direction of the second boat. On the way, it hit a lure being pulled by the other vessel, and the two boats were now connected to the same fish at the same time.

Both captains tried to maximize the leverage of two rods fighting one monstrous fish, but it was useless. The drag on one reel burned up and the one hundred and twenty-pound test line parted. The weary crew on the first boat battled the big one for another three hours before the fish changed directions and charged the boat. The captain gunned both engines to avoid a collision. The fish rocked the boat as it bolted by, and the shaken angler lost his rod overboard as he fell from the fighting chair.

News about "Splash" spread quickly. Surf fishermen from the Pacific coast and boat captains from as far away as Nova Scotia appeared on the coastline. The biggest striper tournament of the year was scheduled to take place over the weekend, and the ruckus over "Splash" had created the entry of more than ten thousand boats.

On day two of the tournament, the captain of the charter boat named "Water Chicken" broke the radio silence. "FISH ON!" was heard across the airways. From the excitement in his voice, everyone knew that "Splash" had been hooked. Fishing boats converged on the area to see the "Water Chicken" fight the striped monster. Linesiders are not known to jump, but this one sent streams of water skyward each time its paddle-like tail pounded the surface. "Chicken John," the boat's Captain, urged other fishermen to stay clear. Those with binoculars viewed the epic battle from afar.

Eighteen hours into the fight, "Splash" showed no signs of tiring. The drag on the big reel began to smoke. Yard after yard of line peeled off until the metal of the spool began to show. "Chicken John" put the engines in full reverse. The tug of war continued until "Splash" appeared to be weakening. Finally, the angler was able to regain line and within minutes, the spool began to fill. Captain "Chicken John" was smiling for the first time since the saga began.

The mate then glanced at the GPS and realized they had been pulled into a restricted military zone. Within minutes, a nuclear submarine surfaced off the stern of the "Water Chicken." Sensing that it was being cornered, the big fish made a beeline toward the sub before the line finally snapped and "Splash" was loose. The free-swimming fish continued on a course headed straight to the sub. The Commander, thinking he was under attack, ordered a laser-guided warhead to be fired. The underwater projectile was on target. The explosion created giant water spouts that spewed water and pieces of "Splash" for miles over the ocean's surface.

The old timer was right when he positively said that the big fish would never be taken on a rod and reel. The "Water Chicken" survived the blast and is plying the ocean today. Captain "Chicken John" has not been seen or heard from since. Rumor has it that he is recovering from fright in an asylum in northwest Idaho.

Be reminded that small fish have ... *LARGE TALES!*

Diehard and Sparky

It was pouring rain when Diehard entered the 24/7 Steak & Egg Restaurant. A dripping puddle formed at his feet as he paused to wipe the water from his eyes. To avoid tracking the water, he sat on a stool near the door of the small restaurant. He quickly realized that the only other person having breakfast was Sparky, a fellow employee from the local truck assembly plant. Sparky's job was to add six or eight spark plugs to every new engine as it passed on the assembly line toward Diehard, whose job it was to install the vehicle's battery.

Diehard greeted Sparky and quickly learned that in spite of the bad weather, fish were biting near the dam. Sparky was also headed in that direction. A lifelong friendship began when the two left the restaurant together on the very wet morning. As things happen, the river came swiftly over the dam that day and all the fish washed downstream. The two friends, however, vowed to fish once a week from then on.

And … fish they did, in good weather and bad. Sparky was leery of bad days, but Diehard insisted that inclement weather was always the best time to fish. On bad days, Sparky ceased to ask whether or not they should go, because Diehard went, regardless. On most days, Sparky ate a hurried breakfast. He always appeared at the restaurant on time, but Diehard would already have had his coffee and be ready to leave.

Sparky often reminded Diehard that some day the weather, or some other factor, would prevent them from fishing. Diehard dismissed these dismal predictions and assured Sparky that nothing would ever stop them from wetting a line. Years passed, and in spite of hurricanes, tornadoes, thunder and lightning, they somehow always managed to fish on the scheduled day. Sparky knew that the law of averages was still in his favor, and that eventually the day would come when a fishing trip wasn't going to happen.

Over time, Diehard accumulated the best foul weather gear available, along with a propane heater to warm his face and hands. He even purchased a 4X4 to assure his arrival at the launch ramp in very bad weather.

On a cold dark morning in mid February, they towed their new Jon boat to a private bass pond. They found the key hidden under a rock, and unlocked the gate to the property.

The aluminum boat bounced on the trailer down the dirt road to the water. This was Diehard's first attempt to launch the new boat in the dark. Sparky jumped out to detach the tie downs and give directions. Diehard slowly backed the rig toward the water's edge. After several unsuccessful attempts to align the trailer with the launch ramp, Diehard became perturbed. Sparky's daunting directions did not help. Diehard finally straightened the rig, and on his next attempt, he impatiently rushed backwards much faster than he should have. With a loud crashing noise, the rig came to an abrupt halt. Diehard jumped from the truck to find Sparky rolling with laughter. "I knew it, I knew it, I knew it!" "Knew what?" Diehard shouted. Sparky's spotlight shone on the frozen pond. The boat and trailer had broken through four inches of ice.

The day of reckoning had finally arrived.

Be reminded that small fish have … *LARGE TALES!*

The Fishin' Boat

The Fishin' Boat is the ultimate fishing machine, designed by fishermen for wealthy fishermen. It has more bells and whistles than a luxury automobile and a far greater price tag. Those who have seen it say they would pay any price to own one.

The boat is stealth-like in appearance. When not running, its silhouette is nearly invisible, an advantage when fishing a secret hole, as other anglers find it nearly impossible to determine its location.

When underway, it glows with a green fluorescent hue and glides on a stream of air with no wake. Sunlight penetrates the hull, which makes it transparent to fish swimming below. Best of all, there is never a noise from waves slapping against the bow. A jet propelled electric trolling motor pushes the boat quietly from place to place.

The Fishin' Boat is equipped with so many viewing screens that one might think he's sitting in the cockpit of a plane. State of the art electronics, including RADAR, DVD, GPS, VHF, AUTO PILOT and FISH FINDERS, are positioned in various locations. Most are located at the helm, but others are strategically placed on the fore and aft casting decks and on either side of the motor cowling.

The 360-degree sonar screen shows fish from as far away as a mile. The unit doesn't transmit the normal "beep" when a fish appears within range. Instead, advanced technology allows a female robot voice to identify the quarry and its precise location. For example, the message might say, "a twenty-pound striper at four o'clock … ten feet down … thirty five feet away … swimming toward the boat at three miles per hour."

A test-drive in The Fishin' Boat reveals that a canopy, similar to that of a fighter jet, encapsulates the fisherman when the engine is started. Seat belts and harnesses automatically secure the passengers, while safety helmets are positioned over each person's head. When the green "all systems go" light illuminates, a light tap on the foot throttle puts the boat in motion. It rises a few inches above the water's surface and hovers until more throttle is applied. The ride is as silky smooth as perhaps a journey on Aladdin's flying carpet would be. Speeds in excess of 100 miles per hour allow for more fishing time.

The ride is only a portion of the story. A new technology surrounds the boat with a magnetic field.

The energized water attracts fish within easy casting distance. The color and type lure is not important. With a sonar fix on a fish, a button is pressed on the side of the reel plate, and the energized fish is drawn toward a magnet at the end of the fishing line.

The actual fighting of the fish occurs in the traditional manner. When the fish eventually surrenders, a stream of air forces it from the water into the live well.

The well is equipped to measure, weigh and identify the species. A computer does a quick calculation, prints the cumulative number of fish caught, the total weight and other pertinent information. Should the fish be a candidate for a citation certificate or a record of some sort, the computer will provide the results. It also advises when a limit has been caught and suggests the release of any fish illegal in size. A sign on the console cautions the boater that the computer must know whether one is fishing in a tournament or fishing for food. A tournament angler would not want his catch to be chilled and killed.

A trailer in reverse is no longer a problem. The boat's GPS guidance system prevents it from straying off the ramp. As the trailer clears the water, the tie downs automatically lock the boat in place. An automatic wash down system then cleans the boat for storage. And finally, a glance inside the built-in cooler reveals the catch has been cleaned, bagged and frozen.

Be reminded that small fish have … *LARGE TALES!*

Catawba Cat II

Charlie walked into the River City Tackle Shop and asked if anyone had seen Catawba Cat. Sam, the owner, nodded that he had not. He told Charlie that the catfish man was off on another adventure and would probably have some interesting tales to tell when he returned.

Charlie commented that he had caught a fifty-two-pound flathead the last time he fished with Catawba. About that time, in walked Catawba Cat. He was dressed in his finest camouflaged clothing. The expression on his face was one of a man with a story to tell. Sam, standing behind the register, rang the ship's bell three times. The signal was for all to gather near the spinner bait section to hear Catawba's latest tale. Within minutes, a crowd had formed and the catfish man began to spin his yarn.

He claimed that since his last visit to the tackle shop, he had actually been on an eventful hunting trip. Ralph, a local rabbit hunter, asked, "What type of hunting trip?" Catawba replied, "It began as a deer hunting trip, but it got more exciting than that." Now, he had everyone's attention.

It seems that a few weeks before deer season opened, his hunting club baited a creek bottom with ears of corn. Each morning, and again at dusk, a herd of deer gathered to feast on the offering.

Opening day found Catawba Cat sitting in a deer stand with his rifle aimed at the corn pile. Near sunrise, he heard what sounded like a herd of deer wading down the creek, and he readied his rifle. The large gray object that appeared in the creek willows was not the deer he expected. The animal was a huge African elephant.

The tackle shop crowd did not believe what they were hearing. "A big eared elephant in the middle of a South Carolina cotton field is totally impossible," shouted Ralph, the rabbit hunter!

Undaunted, Catawba continued his story … he knew his gun was no match for the giant Pachyderm, so he engaged the safety and hunkered down, hoping the elephant would leave. Instead, it stayed to eat corn for what seemed like hours, before it finally decided to turn and tramp its way back toward the creek. Catawba then jumped from the stand and ran back to camp. On the way, he vowed not to say a word to anyone about his experience. He knew nobody would ever believe him.

When everyone was back at camp, the local game warden paid a visit. He checked licenses and inspected the deer hanging from an oak tree. As he was leaving, he asked if anyone had seen a herd of elephants. No one answered, not even Catawba. The warden explained that the adjacent farm property had been leased by a large traveling circus for the animals to exercise and roam. He warned the hunters not to shoot if they should see an elephant or a hippopotamus.

The warden's comments ruined any hope of Catawba making a big impression on his hunting friends. Someone later asked him how many deer he had. He answered that he didn't hunt, but went fishing instead.

Catawba claimed that he caught the biggest catfish ever taken on a rod and reel. He explained that as he was landing the fish, a thunderstorm rolled down the creek. It rained ice pellets the size of a truck's tire and he got pounded. He searched for protection from the storm, but could not find a place to hide. He finally did what any good fisherman would do. He opened the mouth of the catfish and climbed inside until the storm had passed.

Be reminded that small fish have … *LARGE TALES!*

Pond of Dreams

Dr. Fletcher Fishmore originally formulated Oil of La Bass, a cream moisturizer popular with the rich and famous. Its popularity allowed him to invest much of his newfound wealth in a tract of land just off an interstate highway that links the northeast with Florida.

Fishmore's "field of dreams" wasn't a baseball diamond, but a Disney-like chain of lakes. When viewed from above, the lakes resembled the silhouette of a sow-bellied largemouth bass. The lakes were to be stocked with bass so large that each female would outweigh the long-standing record of 22 pounds, 8 ounces. To attain his dream, Fishmore gathered a group of creative marine biologists to bio-engineer a strain of giant hybrid largemouth bass.

It was no coincidence that Fishmore's "Pond of Dreams" was a cast away from Montgomery Lake in South Georgia. You may recall that George Perry caught the world record bass there in 1932, more than seventy years ago.

Bulldozers connected the chain of lakes with a system of canals, locks and dams. Special care was given to create a perfect environment for raising trophy bass. Each lake had its own identity, but each was roughly a half-mile wide and two miles long. Thick vegetation along the banks made fishing from the shore impossible, but provided the perfect habitat for a bass' diet of forage fish, insects, frogs, snakes, birds and small animals.

Television, newspapers and magazines heralded the opening of Fishmore's "Pond of Dreams." Pictures portrayed bass that resembled over-inflated footballs with fins and gills. The nests of spawning bass were the size of a rogue elephant's footprint. A television commercial showed a bass leaping from the water to wrestle a bald eagle from the sky, and another featured Clydesdale size bass pulling a beer wagon across a shallow place in a river.

Ten renowned anglers were selected to compete for the honor of breaking the long-standing world bass record. The rules were simple-one bass per angler, no culling allowed. Each fish brought to the weigh site must be released alive. A one million dollar penalty would be assessed for any dead fish.

On the eve of the big tournament, a fierce storm rolled through the region. Lightning and thunder filled the night sky and the wind and rain blew for hours. By daylight, the storm had passed and a beautiful sunrise signaled the beginning of the event. All national TV networks covered opening festivities. Television trucks and satellite dishes filled the rural South Georgia landscape. Interstate highway traffic was backed up to both state lines.

Anglers were furnished with identical Jon boats, each having a 36-volt trolling motor and an extra large live well. The tournament began at 7:00 a.m. By noon, no fish had been caught. Camera crews became frustrated as the pros continued to fish until dark. Not one fish had been caught from the "Pond of Dreams." The tournament finally ended in a ten-way tie for last place. What would have been a public relations/advertising ploy had ended in disaster.

Disgruntled fishermen and biologists were embarrassed. The next day's headlines read, "Pond of Dreams … a Hoax." The "Pond of Dreams" never officially opened. Fletcher Fishmore's reputation was so tarnished that he disappeared from sight and was not heard from again.

The following week, a Boy Scout, fishing from the bank of a lake a short distance away, caught a thirty-two pound bass. The scout was there to earn a fishing merit badge, when the lunker struck a top water plug.

In the days that followed, the record was broken over and over again by youngsters attending the summer camp. The boys were featured on television talk shows and in popular outdoor magazines.

By summer's end, the fish quit biting, but not before a new record was established. It tipped the scales at an even fifty pounds.

How the bass got into the summer camp lake is anybody's guess. The accepted theory is that a tornado accompanied the big storm, drew the trophy bass out of "Fishmore's Pond," and deposited them in the lake where the scouts were fishing.

Be reminded that small fish have … *LARGE TALES!*

Sea Buoy

Mike and Marty were obsessed with the wonders of the sea. They loved viewing it from the bottom up while scuba diving from a small, faded red runabout. The duo frequented many of the reefs and shipwrecks along the southeast coast. Mike preferred the wrecks off the Carolinas, while Marty loved to explore the clear water coral reefs of Florida.

They were heading offshore one particular morning when they noticed a commotion just east of the inlet. Upon closer inspection, they found the disturbance to be a pod of cobia circling a bobbing sea buoy. The cobia had rounded up a school of "peanut bunker" and were thrashing their way through them for a meal. Mike suggested they try to shoot one of the large cobia with a spear gun. Marty maneuvered the boat to the buoy, but the pounding noise of the boat frightened them, and a clear shot was impossible. Minutes turned into hours, as the two divers became frustrated with their elusive prey.

They finally decided it would be easier to shoot a cobia while standing on the giant buoy. Marty nosed the small red runabout back to the buoy and tied a line to it. Mike, with spear gun in hand, jumped onto the floating structure. Marty joined him, where they payed out fifty feet of line to keep the teetering boat distanced from the circling fish.

Standing on a bobbing, slime-covered sea buoy is no easy task, but Marty and Mike were convinced they had a better chance of hitting a big fish from this vantage point than from the small, red runabout.

A large cobia soon swam into range. Mike eyed the target and readied a shot. Just as he pulled the trigger, a giant sea critter jumped to inhale the big cobia and the spear bulls-eyed the monster in the back.

Mike was jerked off the floating platform and began to experience the tow of his life, while Marty pulled the small boat's fifty feet of line back to the buoy. A passing Coast Guard vessel thought he was stranded and circled to lend assistance.

As the cutter neared, the crew saw that Mike was being pulled toward the Gulf Stream at a high rate of speed. The vessel gave chase, but had difficulty keeping pace with the streaking sea critter. They steamed offshore, gaining only a few yards per mile as they attempted to overtake the quarry. Before long, they were well out to sea and fearful that Mike had drowned in the turbulence of his high-speed tow.

Eventually, the Coast Guard came close enough to see that Mike had become tightly wrapped in the line that connected the speared fish to the gun. His severe arm lacerations left a stream of red in the wake created by the monster.

Mike was near his last breath when the Coast Guard took aim from a cannon on the bow. The only hope was to kill the large sea critter before Mike drowned. As they readied the cannon, a bolt of lightning hit the big fish in the exact spot where the spear had entered its massive body. A clap of thunder followed to herald the demise of the giant critter.

All that remained was an aura of green smoke that hovered above a whirlpool, as the critter slowly sank to the bottom of the sea. Mike was brought from the water by the Coast Guard and later recovered. Both divers were found guilty and were fined for violating a variety of federal fishing, hunting and boating regulations.

The giant sea critter was never seen again.

Be reminded that small fish have … *LARGE TALES!*

Mutt & Jeff

Mutt and Jeff had been friends since high school. They began fishing for bass on the river, but switched to crappie fishing after the dam was built. Over the years, they cut down trees and dropped them in different areas of the lake to create brush piles.

The agreement they had was that if they worked together to build a fishing hole, it belonged to both of them to use only when they fished together. If one built his own brush pile, it was to be his and his alone. The holes they shared produced plenty of table fare and enough crappie to win several tournaments.

The two were so competitive that they eventually developed a strong distrust for each other. Neither wanted the other to gain the upper hand. As time passed, Jeff began to suspect that Mutt was fishing on his brush piles. Each time Jeff questioned the fact, Mutt gave him a sheepish grin and shook his head as if to deny it. Jeff grew more and more suspicious.

One spring morning, Jeff rented a small plane and flew over the lake. His suspicions were proven true when he not only found Mutt fishing one of his brush piles, but the rascal had someone fishing with him. Jeff was furious that now someone else would know of his favorite crappie holes.

He decided to say nothing while he plotted a way to get even. Near the end of the crappie season, a weekend tournament had been scheduled. At the last minute, he informed Mutt that he planned to fish the tournament alone.

Mutt was in a state of shock. This was the only tournament the two of them had not fished together since they were kids. Since Mutt didn't want a new partner to learn of his crappie holes either, he also opted to fish alone. His first spot was void of fish, as were the second, third, and forth. This had never happened to him.

As the day continued, Mutt noticed that his eyes began to blur. Soon, he was actually having trouble seeing. Why were his eyes watering each time he stopped to fish? Could it be foul play?

He finally had to stop fishing and head for the weigh-site. By the time he arrived, his eyes were very red and tears were streaming down his face. The weigh master thought he was crying because he had no fish.

Jeff won the crappie tournament with a new record of ten fish that weighed twenty-eight pounds. Mutt's tears continued to flow. Tournament anglers taunted him, and jeered that he was crying because he had lost the tournament.

On the way home, he stopped at a local produce market for some tomatoes and onions. The clerk informed him that all the onions had been sold the day before. It seems that someone had filled an entire truck with burlap sacks full of yellow onions.

A mile from home, Mutt solved the problem about his teary eyes. Jeff had contaminated his thirty crappie holes with the thirty sacks of yellow onions.

Be reminded that small fish have … *LARGE TALES!*

Rawhide Part II

Fishing hasn't been the same for Rawhide since the concussion he sustained at the weigh-in of that big striper tournament a few years ago. You may recall that he won the tourney with an eighty-pound striper. After the accident, he couldn't remember where he had caught the big fish.

He spent many fishing trips trying to relocate the spot his ancestors referred to as the "Happy Fishing Grounds." He didn't earn a single top ten finish in thirty-four tournaments. Most days, he didn't even catch a legal size fish. Once the proudest of all fishermen, his reputation gradually faded, and he was fast becoming a broken man. He began to think long and hard about moving to the other side of the mountains where stripers were rumored to be big and much easier to catch.

One day, he and his wife, Fran, jumped in the white family pickup truck and headed across the mountain range to take a look. What they saw was a new beginning, a chance for Rawhide to re-establish himself as a formidable striper fisherman.

On the return trip, they stopped at an Indian reservation where they met the tribe's Grand Chief. Rawhide and the Grand Chief hit it off from the start. Both had ancestors who had hunted wild buffalo on the open plains of the old west.

Seated crossed-legged at the campfire that evening, Rawhide confided in the Grand Chief. He explained what he could remember about his secret striper honey hole. The old Indian offered him a puff from a ceremonial cigar. It might have been the aroma of the cigar's tobacco, but for whatever the reason, Rawhide began to feel better than he had in many moons. The chief promised to meditate over Rawhide's memory loss. He vowed to offer a solution by the time the sun rose over the mountaintop the next morning.

Rawhide couldn't sleep. Visions of trophy stripers danced through his head all night. When morning finally came, the Grand Chief offered his advice and then disappeared into his gift shop. Rawhide pondered the meaning of the Indian's words, "Look to the sky."

The following day found Rawhide on his home lake at dawn. Instead of watching his depth finder, he spent hours staring into the Carolina Blue sky. Day after day he looked to the sky, but saw nothing. He was now without a win in thirty-seven tournament events. His thoughts again turned to Tennessee, where stripers were big and easy to catch. After months of indecision, he and Fran decided to make their move. The lake house went on the market and they were going to the Volunteer State.

Before leaving, Rawhide had one final tournament to redeem himself. He awakened early on that day to find the lake covered by a heavy blanket of fog. He despondently thought to himself that if he couldn't catch fish on a clear day, how the heck would he find them in the fog?

He was launching the boat when he heard a shrill sound coming from the foggy sky. He quickly lowered his electric trolling motor and followed the noise. It seemed like hours had passed, when something finally crashed into the water. The fog had lifted barely enough to see a huge eagle fly away with a twenty-pound striper.

Rawhide hit the waypoint button on his new GPS unit to mark the exact spot. Immediately, he began to fish, thinking all the while that the Grand Chief's prophecy had just come true. Before his bait reached the bottom, his rod doubled over and then shattered into several pieces. Whatever it was, hit with the force of a spaceship moving at warp speed.

The fog lifted before Rawhide could lower another bait. Much to his amazement, he realized that he was on his secret striper honey hole in the middle of the "Happy Fishing Grounds." He recognized the spot by the bubbles that rose from the bottom and by the sight of the many stripers flashing just below the surface. He was so happy that he actually threw his best fishing rod into the water and did a one legged fish dance! He then proceeded to light the unused portion of his ceremonial cigar, a gift from the Grand Chief.

As he puffed away, a striper of monstrous proportions hit his bait. While he reeled in the huge fish, he happily hummed the words, "Glory, glory, Hallelujah!" He skillfully fought and netted the giant fish on the first pass. It was larger than any he had ever seen or heard about.

At the weigh-in, Rawhide was the sentimental favorite. Everybody was rooting for him to win his last tournament. When it came his turn to weigh his catch, a shrill noise came from the sky and shattered the silence of the moment. The crowd peered upward to see a bald eagle tip its wings.

As they cheered, Rawhide took his big fish to the scales. The people were overjoyed. Mothers threw babies into the air and grown men did back flips. They knew that the tournament winner would not be moving to Tennessee.

While giving his victory speech, Rawhide saw the Grand Chief standing on a nearby hill with the eagle perched on his shoulder. When asked where he caught the big striped bass, Rawhide smiled, puffed on his cigar and said, "M-11."

Be reminded that small fish have … *LARGE TALES!*

Catawba Cat and Deere Jon

Catawba Cat, the famous fisherman, is the half-brother of an equally well known hunter named Deere Jon, who tracks and kills thousand pound hogs, traps blue tailed foxes, golden wolves and albino coyotes. Some may recall a story that appeared in a popular duck-hunting magazine about Deere Jon's adventures while hunting waterfowl near Jane Fonda's plantation in coastal South Carolina.

Last May the brothers had a rare opportunity to fish together. They met at a fish camp on Santee Cooper. Catawba, hoping to impress Deere Jon, began the fishing trip by suggesting that they try the diversion channel for a few mullet to use as bait. They left the camp with snatch hooks on ten-pound test spinning outfits.

The first mullet Deere Jon snagged took off like a scalded wildcat and broke the line before it had traveled fifteen feet. Catawba went to his truck for a twenty-pound rig. A large mullet soon broke it.

The only tackle left to try was the eighty-pound gear that Catawba had used to catch his world record catfish. It was too heavy to cast, so he slung the big gang hook into the channel and began to reel. Within minutes, he had half a dozen mullet of various sizes up to thirty-six pounds. It was then that he suggested they go sturgeon fishing. Deere Jon's reaction was, "Sturgeon in South Carolina? Give me a break!"

Catawba assured him that some of the largest of all freshwater fish in Santee Cooper were sturgeons. He related rumors about the Department of Natural Resources stocking "Russian Olympic Sturgeon" in the lower lake during the late

1940's. Catawba suspected that they should be really large by now, maybe even up to a thousand pounds.

After some persuasion by Catawba, he and Deere Jon took their tub of mullet to the deep water near the power plant. Catawba tail-hooked a mullet and lobbed it as far away from the bank as he could. The twenty-pound mullet splashed like a striper as it took the line and headed toward Charleston Harbor.

It didn't get far before a gigantic explosion sent a plume of water thirty feet into the air. Deere Jon set the hook and held tightly to the rod. The unknown prey splashed time after time, but never cleared the water enough that they could tell what was hooked. Catawba hoped it was a sturgeon, but all he knew for sure was that Deere Jon had never seen a larger animal on any of his hunting trips.

As afternoon turned to night, the epic battle continued. At sunrise the following morning, the fish with scales the size of giant Moon Pies, appeared to be tiring as it came closer to the bank. The fury in its eyes was apparent when it spotted Deere Jon at the other end of the line. Catawba stabbed it with a gaff and it rolled over.

The episode did not end with the gaffed fish. It continued to roll until it yanked the gaff from Catawba's hands and created a loud explosion. The noise occurred when Deere Jon's eighty-pound test line broke. The fish swirled once again before disappearing below the surface.

When the waters had settled, Catawba examined the remaining end of the parted line. The last thirty feet were coated with globs of dripping catfish slime.

A state biologist confirmed the catch. Deere Jon lost what would have been a new world record blue catfish. The monster was thought to have exceeded a thousand pounds.

Most anglers considered the tale of the battle to be another of Catawba's yarns. The fact that catfish don't have scales the size of giant Moon Pies, added to their suspicions. Catawba counters the disbelievers by informing them that "eating-size catfish don't have scales, but thousand pounders do."

Be reminded that small fish have ... *LARGE TALES!*

Gold Mine Bass

Wally and Ken became excited when they heard that a bass tournament would take place on a nearby lake. The fishing duo had spent many hours getting tackle ready to pre-fish the big event.

They explored areas at the far north side of the lake they had never fished before. It was there that they discovered a waterfall. The base of the fall was loaded with three to five pound feisty bass that hit anything cast in their direction.

On tournament day, boats from the entire region waited patiently for the flare to signal the blast off. Wally and Ken stayed back to prevent other boats from following them to the secret spot.

Upon their arrival, they were disappointed to find that boats were already fishing the falls. They watched sadly as bass after bass was taken from the water at the base of the cascade. Four hours later, the bite slowed and one by one the boats moved off to fish other parts of the impoundment.

The youthful pair seized the opportunity and motored to the exact spot where bass had been plentiful the week before. Unfortunately, the other fishermen had either caught or scared away the reminder of the fish. With no bites, they finally became disgusted and decided to try another spot.

As they pulled away, Ken pointed to what appeared to be a cave behind the waterfall. With fishing rods in hand, they motored to the area. The river that ran through the cave was full of bass. It wasn't long before both anglers were catching fish. In the semi-darkness, they noticed a golden sparkle on the drops of water shed by the jumping bass.

The boys quickly caught the limit and headed toward the cave opening. Ken lifted the lid of the live well to view the catch. What they saw boggled their minds so much that they skipped the tournament weigh-in and headed home. When the boat was safely behind the closed garage door, they opened the live well to re-inspect their haul.

The bottom of the live well was covered with gold. The tongues and gills of the bass were coated with flakes of gold. They collected two sandwich size baggies full of gold flakes. The next day, the boys skipped school and headed back to the falls.

On this morning, they left the rods and reels at home and loaded the boat with picks and shovels.

Be reminded that small fish have … *LARGE TALES!*

Firedrake

It had been an unusually hot and humid summer. The combination of heat and moisture made the lake foggy every evening.

Beginning sometime in early July, frantic phone calls flooded the 911 switchboards. Each report was the same. Callers saw flames coming from beneath the water and shooting into the sky. Responding firemen, search and rescue workers, and law enforcement officers found nothing. Rumors of a medieval-like fire-breathing dragon eventually slowed tourism to a trickle. Year round residents ceased to fish, swim, and cruise the lake.

It appeared that a "Loch Ness" story was developing. Reporters, film crews, and scientists from around the country filled the summer cottages left vacant by frightened tourists. Planes, boats and submersibles scoured the lake for signs of the so-called "Firedrake." Reports persisted, but by the end of the summer season, authorities had not confirmed a single sighting. Even the local parson vowed on a stack of Bibles that he had observed fire spewing into the sky from the waters of his cove.

As summer quickly turned to fall, the locals remained and the furor subsided. Deer and rabbit hunters filled the forests that surrounded the once tranquil lake. Then a new report surfaced about a fire-breathing dragon. This time, the sightings came from a deep pool in a creek that flowed into the lake. A hunter, sitting in a deer stand, saw big flames shooting from the pool. He surmised that the "Firedrake" had moved upstream to avoid being found by the monster hunters.

The new report accelerated the search and once again, officials were baffled. They desperately wished for the so-called "Firedrake" to move on before the beginning of another tourist season.

The first Saturday of April reluctantly brought everyone to the water's edge to fish for trout. Legend had it that if you missed opening day, ten years of bad luck would follow. Minutes into the new season, the first of many sightings of red and blue flames shot into the morning sky. Anglers backed away each time another flame appeared. Not a single trout was caught that morning. By mid-day, the banks were empty. It was as though an evil spell had been cast over the lake village. Everyone feared the worst. The following morning, the good parson prayed for mercy as the wary congregation shouted, "Amen!"

Monday was a school holiday. Children spent the day skipping stones across the lake. A trail of sparks followed the slick rocks as they skidded across the surface. The following day, the kids related their experience to the science teacher. After school, the teacher hustled to the lake to throw rocks. He discovered that the larger the rock, the brighter the spark. When very large rocks hit the surface, sparks became flames. The science teacher had seen enough.

Sirens sounded at 12:00 PM the next day to signal an evacuation order. As the town folks retreated to high ground, helicopters were heard coming over the mountain. The military choppers, ten in all, began dropping three-ton sandbags into the lake. Their hope was to get the Firedrake so excited that he would overheat and explode. With bomb-like sandbags falling from the sky and fire spewing from the water below, the lake resembled a war zone.

A shroud of smoke had covered the lake, when a tremendous explosion jolted the region. The chopper crews that hovered above saw what looked like pieces of shrapnel shooting skyward. The all-clear siren sounded at sunset.

The next day found the landscape covered with bits and pieces of what appeared to be the body parts of a monster. Since no one had ever seen a real Firedrake, the green and reddish samples were sent to a laboratory. Tests confirmed body parts of an undetermined origin. The carbon dating analysis showed the suspected Firedrake to be approximately three hundred eighty-five years old.

How it got into the lake is anybody's guess. Rumors of settlers from Europe in the early 1600's, tell of bringing bird, fish and reptile eggs to the New World. Maybe one of the eggs was that of a Firedrake?

Be reminded that small fish have … *LARGE TALES!*

Land Sharks

It was the biggest weekend of the summer on the Grand Strand, but the beach was empty. Not one umbrella could be seen. Fearsome sharks had taken up residence at the ocean's edge. Known as "land sharks," the critters had created a ghost town from what was once the most popular seacoast vacation spot in the Carolinas.

Photo of a sign Gus found at a store in coastal North Carolina.

Thousands of dorsal fins replaced the bobbing heads of bathers along a hundred-mile stretch of beach. The sharks could not only swim, but were capable of maneuvering their way onto the beach to lie in ambush, partially covered with sand. No one knew for sure where the sharks came from, but the popular consensus was perhaps from an inland sea on the other side of the ocean, maybe Africa. They first appeared after a tropical storm had devastated the beach resort.

They weren't as large as the man-eating sharks we know about, but were big enough to take a chunk out of an arm or leg. At first, small dogs and house pets disappeared. Then a horde of bloody victims with bites and missing extremities filled emergency rooms. A reign of terror and panic engulfed the beach resort. A rumor quickly spread that an infant on a beach blanket was dragged into the ocean by a golden shark. The mother went berserk when her first-born disappeared into the frothing surf.

Satellite photos, heat-seeking laser equipment and mine detectors could not locate the stealth like "land sharks." Flat tires were a common occurrence any time a four wheel drive Humvee or military style jeep ventured onto the sand. One beach buggy received four flat tires as it topped a dune near the old Pavilion. Sand-whacking land sharks had learned to disable beach vehicles by nipping at the sidewalls when they rolled by. Fearing a shark attack, the patrolling officers leaped from the buggy and made a mad dash across the barren sands to the safety of the boardwalk.

A few days before the Labor Day weekend, the once bustling beach community was hit with another horrific event. A thunderstorm dropped twenty-four inches of rain in less than two hours. Streets and shops were filled with water, and the fins of cruising sharks were seen on Main Street. Over time, the water receded and the sharks returned to their stronghold on the very deserted beach.

The town hired a New England firm that specialized in exterminating sharks. The company was owned and operated by the son of the immortal shark fisherman, Captain Quint. You may recall that Capt. Quint was the "old salt" that died while attempting to rid the mythical town of Amity from a bothersome great white shark. The young Quint had never seen anything like this. His experience had led him to tackle one big shark at a time, not thousands of the toothy critters.

Quint was walking the boardwalk when he noticed a youngster sitting atop a sand dune. Apparently, he had wandered away from his parents and was playing with some small objects in the sand. Fearing for the boy's life, Quint ran to his aide. There, he noticed humps in the sand that indicated the presence of "land sharks." To his surprise, the sharks were fortunately quite distanced from the dune top and he was able to sweep the child to safety.

The boy's playthings gave Quint an idea that put his shark eradication plan into action. The following day, thousands of trucks dumped their cargo on the sand dunes at high tide. When the tide receded, the piles disappeared. The dump trucks returned to leave load after load at each high tide. The truck parade continued for days.

In mid September, the young Quint called a press conference. He announced that the "land sharks" were gone, and that it was safe to use the beach again. During the question and answer portion of the conference, Quint was asked, "What was in the dump trucks?" His response was, "The dump trucks were unloading what the little boy was playing with, only many more of them." "And what was that?" His reply was, "hermit crabs." It seems that the millions of feisty little crabs, when set loose, nipped and bit the sandy hides of the "land sharks" much the same way as mosquitoes aggravate humans. It became so unbearable for them that eventually they left the beach. They never returned.

Next time you swim at the beach, thank a Hermit Crab.

Be reminded that small fish have … *LARGE TALES!*

The Lying Schoolboy

The schoolboy didn't have to lie, but he did. He lied every time he mentioned anything about fishing. He even stretched the truth when he caught fish in great numbers and record sizes. He meant nothing by the lies; it was merely a way of life to him.

He was excused early from school one afternoon because he claimed to be sick. The only illness he had was the "Fishin' Pox." From the schoolyard, he rode his bike home, stopping only long enough to grab his fishing pole. With rod in hand, he hightailed it to the dock of the bay.

Conditions were perfect; the tide was in, and the fish were biting. The lying boy made ten casts and landed ten fish. None were very large, but were a nice size for that time of year. Time passed that day, until brother Buddy came to the dock and beckoned Billy home. They hustled down the road, late for dinner again.

Miraculously, the ten fish became one hundred and twenty at school the next day. They also grew in size overnight. The principal overheard the story—even the part when Billy bragged about catching a seventeen-pound trout the afternoon before. The schoolmarm didn't believe the part about the seventeen-pounder, but she knew the fishing trip was true. Billy was ushered to the main office, read the riot act, and was suspended until Monday. His parents were called to take him home.

This "teller of tall tales" spent the rest of the evening in his bedroom. The following day, he was given explicit instructions to remain at home and study. Study he did, but only long enough for his parents to leave the driveway. He then jumped on his bike and headed back to his fishing hole.

Fishing was so good that he told on himself when his father came home that evening. Billy mistakenly bragged about catching an eight-foot giant of a barracuda that leaped more than a hundred times. He was sent back to his room for another evening of solitary confinement.

Billy continued to fish and lie about what he caught. All the while, he honed his skills as an angler. Years passed and nothing changed. Billy fished and lied, fished and lied and fished and lied some more. The only time this modern day Pinocchio wasn't telling lies was when his mouth wasn't moving. He lied so much that his friends didn't believe a word he said, and most of them stopped hanging out and fishing with him.

A big fishing tournament was scheduled for the weekend. No one would fish with the biggest liar in the world, so he fished alone, and boy did he catch fish! When it came his turn to weigh his catch, he had to have a couple of guys help him carry his big cooler to the scales. Before opening the cooler, he took the microphone and began to spin a tale about his battle most of the day, with a very large fish. Following this tale was one of an even larger fish that also got away.

On the third yarn, the crowd began to boo and chant, "Weigh your fish, weigh your fish!" This time he claimed that he hooked a monster so big that it almost pulled him out to sea. The crowd became more and more belligerent as he continued to tell one tale after another. They even began to throw fish heads and rotten bait at the unpopular orator.

Sensing the hostility, he went to his ice chest and pulled out a fifty-pound fish. Even though the fish was a nice one, the crowd had already seen several fish that weighed in at over one hundred pounds. They booed again. Billy raised his arms and shouted to the boisterous crowd, "This was my bait!" With that, a tow truck big enough to haul an eighteen-wheeler, drove to the front of the stage. A hush fell over the crowd as the boos quickly turned to cheers.

Billy had a big smile on his face when he accepted the grand prize. The crowd left the tournament singing, "For He's a Jolly Good Fellow." Hanging from the hook of the tow truck was a super grouper that Billy appropriately named "Kong."

As time passed, "Kong" grew in size, as did all of Billy's fish. His most recent recollection is that the fish was so big, it flipped the tow truck over backwards and the super grouper was crushed before it was ever weighed. Billy was sure that it would have bottomed out on the scales at ten thousand pounds. That's a lot of fish sandwiches!

Be reminded that small fish have … *LARGE TALES!*

The First Fishing Guide

Cavemen were hunters by trade. They tracked giant dinosaurs twenty-four/seven and seldom took any time off. In fact, hunting was not a sport, as we know it today, but was very hard work. Think about it! How much fun would it be to kill a Tyrannosaurus Rex and have to drag it for miles back to a cave?

As time passed and the men tired of the hunt, some became artists of sorts. Paintings are preserved on walls of caves around the world. Even when the caveman took an infrequent day off, life was boring without television, football and NASCAR. The hunter stayed holed-up in his cave and sharpened spears and axe heads for the next day's hunt.

One day a tall slender caveman named Lur, found himself standing at the edge of a mist-covered sea. Until that moment, the only water he had ever seen flowed in a brook that ran near his one room cave.

Lur threw his club at a low flying winged reptile and missed. The club landed in the water with a big splash. The commotion frightened a school of fierce looking fish. One jumped up onto the bank and landed at Lur's feet. He grabbed the flopping fish with both hands, but it slipped away and swam back out to sea.

Lur was quite excited. He hurried back to Caveville and articulated his tale. Articulate might be a poor choice of words, but the language of the day consisted mainly of grunts, groans and a few hand and face motions. His tale became the first fish story ever told. Lur claimed that the fish he called "Bas," were larger than any Zorrontosuarus-X that ever roamed the planet. The clansmen listened with interest.

The following morning, the cavemen threw rocks and sticks into the sea, hoping to duplicate Lur's experience, but the "Bas" had either disappeared or were not jumping that day. As the men walked back to Caveville, the elder clansman, a man named Rod, grunted, "I guess we should have been here yesterday."

That evening, the cavemen gathered around a fire to eat the remains of a wild chicken. Two brawny cavemen fought over the breast and broke it at the wishbone. The next day, Lur found the broken wishbone and took it with him to the water's edge. He baited it with a chunk of dinosaur meat and cast it into the sea. Unknowingly, Lur had invented the first fishhook. The best was yet to come!

A fish took the bait and Lur hauled it to shore. This time he was able to hold on to the slippery "Bas." Lur spent the remainder of the day bragging about his catch and showing it off. That night he cooked it over the cave fire. One of the so-called "artists" painted a rendering of Lur's bass on his cave wall. The picture lives in history and symbolizes what was to be the beginning of man's favorite sport—bass fishing. Word spread quickly that fish were fun and easy to catch, and were much tastier than dinosaurs.

Finally, Lur ceased to hunt and he became the world's first fishing guide. He fished by day and made hooks by night. The other cavemen held him in high esteem. He had given them a reason to enjoy life. "Bas Fishin'" became Caveville's favorite pastime.

Lur befriended the artist who painted the fish on the walls of his cave. The artist became well known to other cavemen who soon came from near and far to view his works. Caveville became the beginning of what would be known as the Fishin' Age. Steady streams of tourists lined the mountain to view the fish art inside the cave.

Many years later, pictures were drawn on T-shirts in a theme park that featured a mouse that fished with a goofy looking dog.

The fishing business prospered. Lur's Fishing Guide Service is still in existence. Only the name has been changed to … "Fishin' With Capt. Gus!"

Be reminded that small fish have … *LARGE TALES!*

Ringo, the Cell Phone Fisherman

Everyone calls Ringo. He gets so many phone calls that he had to get an 800 number. No, Ringo is not a famous band member, but a local fisherman and a pretty good one at that. His cell phone rings constantly. When it isn't ringing, it's because he's already talking to someone. Ringo is on the phone even when he's fishing from his center console boat. He talks very loud because cell phone reception on the lake is poor, at best.

Even with "call waiting," Ringo has to interrupt one conversation to talk to another caller. Back and forth he goes between callers. Once he tried to use three phones, but that proved to be a mess. It worked best to use only one, a deluxe phone with a picture on the screen of the fish that didn't get away.

Ringo claims that most phone calls occur when he is playing a fish. He finally bought one of those new fangled earphones that allowed him to fish and talk at the same time. The only problem was that when his hands were wet, he heard a loud buzz in the headpiece. It buzzed so much one day that he threw the phone in the lake. That proved to be a big mistake.

Within minutes, all the fish in the cove came to the surface. They were stunned as if they had been electrocuted. Fish were splashing everywhere. Ringo thought it was pretty cool at first, and then he realized that it was illegal to shock fish. A passing angler saw the flipping fish and called Wildlife Enforcement. An officer arrived immediately to question Ringo. He was transported to a local jail where the jail keeper, a staunch conservationist, was appalled by Ringo's evil deed.

As the jail door slammed shut, Ringo saw a sign on the wall that read … "NO CELL PHONES ALLOWED."

Be reminded that small fish have … *LARGE TALES!*

Fishcoy

Deere Jon invited Catawba Cat, his half brother, to join him on a "fish hunt" in LA. Catawba Cat thought Los Angeles seemed like a strange place to fish and a "fish hunt" didn't sound right either. What the heck, he would go for the fun of it.

Ready for the "Fish-Hunt"

At the appointed time, Deere Jon's dirty red pickup rolled into the driveway. The truck's bed was loaded with fishing gear, ice chests, several large duffle bags, and Jon's favorite double-barreled shotgun. A green and white polka dot handkerchief was tied to the end of the pirogue that slanted skyward over the tail-gate. Sitting in the passenger seat was a young Labrador retriever that Deere Jon called Doe. The dog's full pedigreed name was Doe-a-Deere. Catawba Cat didn't quite know what to expect about a "fish hunt" with a dog named Doe and man named Deere.

He threw his stuff in the back of the truck and jumped in the cab. The pickup bounced the threesome down the highway in a south-west direction. After several hours, Deere Jon stopped in front of a doublewide that was old, silver and rusty. The aging beauty sat on a muddy creek bank near a little town named Foley. "This is it!" Brother Deere said, as his boots hit the Ala-bama dirt. A confused Catawba Cat suddenly found himself, not in Los Angeles, but in lower Alabama, for a weekend of "fish hunting."

The following morning, the half brothers threw all sizes and colors of fishcoys into the waters of a shallow marsh. The larger ones resembled largemouth bass, and the others looked a lot like bream and crappie. Doe-a-Deere supervised the positioning of the fishcoys from her vantage point in the bed of the pickup truck.

The trio waited a very long time, but nothing happened. Brother Deere tried using the fish caller he had received as a Christmas present. Catawba Cat was leery. He thought he was being tricked and couldn't decide whether he was hunting or fishing. The last time he felt this way was when he was left holding the bag on a midnight snipe hunt.

The fishcoys were left in the water overnight in hopes of attracting a school in the dark. The next morning, Deere Jon was the first to reach the marsh. He found the fishcoys on the other side. One was bobbing up and down like something was holding it. He jumped into his pirogue and poled toward the wayward fishcoys. When he was almost there, he reached for the one that was bobbing. It went under, only to resurface a few feet away. Jon whistled and the water exploded. Doe had jumped in to encounter the unknown creature. The water and the fury blinded Jon.

When his eyes cleared enough to see, he began to swing his push pole at the creature. It leaped from the water and knocked him from the pirogue. The battle was wild. Finally, Jon heard Catawba Cat's voice screaming, "Stop, it's me, it's me!"

It seems that Catawba Cat had awakened early, discovered that the fishcoys hadn't attracted anything, and he waded into the dark water to move them. He had moved all but one, when he became entangled in the line of the one that resembled a big bass. That's when Deere Jon arrived and saw it bobbing across the marsh.

But, that's not the end of the tale. The local game warden appeared while the exhausted brothers were collecting the fishcoys. Somehow, the warden could not be convinced that they were fishing, and not hunting. The fishcoys looked too much like decoys to him. Not only that, but Doe-a-Deere appeared to be there for a reason, and the shotgun in the truck certainly looked suspicious. The officer whisked them off to the Foley, Alabama courthouse where the presiding judge found the brothers guilty of hunting out of season without a license.

Be reminded that small fish have … *LARGE TALES!*

Mac's Daydream

Mac, the lake's premier Catfish Guide, left his boat dock and headed to a stump filled creek. The trip upriver was uneventful, with only the noise of a few cackling crows heard over the hum of the four-stroke engine.

Upon arrival at his favorite fishing hole, Mac readied four rigs. Two were baited with perch filets, the other two with bream heads. The lines were cast, and the trolling motor was on autopilot. Mac sat back to relax and enjoy the morning with hopes of a few nice cats for dinner.

Fifteen minutes later, he brought a small channel cat to the boat, and then a small blue. One after another, he landed dozens of whiskered catfish, which made him wonder if he would have enough bait to last the trip. Just as he was thinking about moving to a spot that might hold larger fish, a big one tugged violently on his line, and the rod bent toward the water.

Mac quickly pulled the rod from its holder. The fish pulled line from the reel and the drag sang from the pressure. Mac said to himself, "Self, I'm glad my new outfit was filled with heavy duty line." As he said that, the fish began to really take off, and didn't stop until it had taken one hundred feet of line. It then began to slowly circle the boat. Mac didn't think it was ever going to stop. It had been hooked for so long that he began to fantasize about being Santiago, the Cuban fisherman who hooked the giant marlin in Hemingway's "Old Man and The

Sea." All Mac could think about was landing the fish, weighing it, and spending the rest of his life bragging about catching it!

The fish finally stopped circling, made another run, and stopped. The rod bent double, but the fish would not budge. As in the novel, it was man against beast. Mac began to wonder who had who.

A few minutes later, a second rod had a hit. The old rod went down even more violently than the first one. "Stay with the fish," Mac said to himself. He loosened the drag and let the second fish swim freely. Mac's restful fishing trip had turned into quite a morning. His legs were shaking; he was sweating, and becoming very tired from the fight. He even began to question himself. How could he land two fish, when one was more than he could handle?

He called upon his years of experience and applied renewed pressure to the line. Thinking he might be hung on a brush pile, he motored toward the fish. When his line was tight, he felt a tug. The fish broke free from the hang-up and resumed the battle.

Mac saw bubbles rising to the surface, a sign that the fish was finally being defeated. He scrambled for his biggest net, and somehow the monster cat swam straight into it. The net stretched and the handle bowed from the weight, as he struggled to get the creature into the boat. He heaved a great sigh of relief when the battle was won. He had landed the largest catfish ever taken on a rod and reel.

As he worked the big cat from the net, he noticed that there were two hooks in its mouth. Apparently, it was so big that it never realized it was hooked when it bit the second bait.

The fish was much too large to weigh on Mac's hand held scales, or to fit in the cooler or the live well. He released the fish with no photos, no one to vouch for its size, and no one to authenticate the catch.

So how big was the fish? Mac claimed it weighed one thousand, one hundred and one pounds, plus one ounce. "How did you make that calculation?" someone asked. Mac shook his head and yawned as he awakened from his mid-afternoon nap.

Be reminded that small fish have … *LARGE TALES!*

The Light House

This saga begins as a crusty old salt named Blacky climbed the steps the first time to light the beacon atop the lighthouse. The red and white striped pinnacle is well known by mariners who ply the coastline off Fishtauga.

Blacky is the fifth keeper in the past three years to man the light and the only applicant for the job. The others all mysteriously disappeared. No one wanted to be the lighthouse keeper.

Blacky's weird behavior had everyone puzzled. The townspeople thought it was strange that he wore a black silk stovepipe hat everywhere he went. Rumor has it that he even wore it to bed.

Weird too, was that he spent most of his daylight hours walking around the light in a counterclockwise direction. Coincidently, a pod of sharks always circled in a clockwise motion. Why, was anyone's guess? It is safe to surmise that Blacky didn't want the toothy critters sneaking up behind him, so he walked facing them.

So it went, man and beast circled the light in different directions day after day. To anyone else, the ritual might have been boring, but Blacky looked forward to the exercise and enjoyed watching the sharks swim by.

One afternoon, a large bull shark poked his head from the water and showed a mouthful of menacing teeth. Undaunted, Blacky began to take a long handled harpoon with him each time he strolled around the lighthouse. Over time, he and the shark became sparring partners, each vying for his own territory.

The shark swam and finned closer and closer to the lighthouse shoreline and showed his sharp pearly whites with increased frequency. The hostility grew, but neither backed down. Blacky enjoyed taunting the shark by prodding it with the harpoon when it came too close. The dangerous game continued for months. Blacky viewed it as a harmless pastime.

One night, the beacon didn't come on at sunset. "It's haunted!" shouted a patron from the local pub. Blacky's brother was at the other end of the bar. Upon hearing the news, he sobbed, "He's gone. He's gone."

The next morning a supply boat was dispatched to search for Blacky. The boat captain scoured every corner of the lighthouse. An eerie feeling came over him when he spotted a thousand or more circling sharks. He began to fear for his life, and left. He found giant shark teeth along the path that led him to the dock.

As he boarded his boat, he saw something very strange headed in his direction. He hustled to untie the lines and was well underway before turning to see if the "something" was following him. What he saw in the wake was the biggest bull shark he had ever seen. What was so unusual? A black silk top hat was riding on its dorsal fin.

Be reminded that small fish have … *LARGE TALES!*

Great White ... A True Story

We were eating dinner at the Lone Cedar Restaurant in Nags Head during a weekend fishing trip to North Carolina's outer banks. Our group included Captain Craig Price, Captain Lindy Sikes, Mike Bradshaw and yours truly, Captain Gus Gustafson.

Seated at the next table, three couples were enjoying the cool spring evening. One of the ladies in the group asked if we were striper fishing the following morning. We answered, "Yes, with Capt. Shannon Miller aboard the 'Blood Vessel.'" She invited us to join her group in the lounge when we had completed our meal.

We joined our new acquaintances. Capt. Donnie Braddick was a member of this group of locals. He is the master of a commercial fishing vessel, "The Bobalou," which long lines for tuna, swordfish, sharks and mahi-mahi. Long lining, as the word implies, is a very long fishing line that stretches for miles. It is the salt-water version of a trotline, the rig used to catch catfish in fresh water lakes and rivers.

Captain Braddick had just returned from a successful fishing trip. He and friends were celebrating "The Bobalou's" big catch.

We learned that Braddick holds the unofficial record for the largest fish ever caught on a rod and reel anywhere in the world. He caught the 3,427-pound, seventeen-foot great white shark, while fishing with Capt. Frank Mundus off Montauk Point, NY in 1986. Some say that Capt. Frank Mundus was the inspiration for Captain Quint, the crusty shark fisherman in the movie, "Jaws." The monstrous fish would have been an International Game Fish Association world record if it hadn't been for a technicality.

The great white was baited with a chunk of blubber carved from the carcass of a whale that the shark pack was feasting upon. Once hooked, the fish was subdued in less than three hours, which is quick, and speaks highly of Braddick's skill and of the other professional fishermen that day aboard the "Cricket III."

As it turned out, the biggest problem they had was when the crew tried to weigh the fish. It was so heavy that the first attempt to raise it from the water shredded the tail. Eventually a cargo net was used to hoist it to the scales.

Capt. Braddick told us that the giant shark he captured was not the biggest one he saw that day. He believed that another shark running with the hungry pack, possibly weighed over four thousand pounds.

Meeting the man who had landed the largest fish ever caught on rod and reel was like shaking hands with the legendary driver of the number 3 stock car. In fact, Captain Braddick's great white shark and Dale Earnhardt's black racecar had something in common. They both weighed approximately thirty five hundred pounds.

Be reminded that small fish have … *LARGE TALES!*

In December of 2005, Captain Gus published the following Christmas message to his readers:

A Visit from Captain Gus

"T'was the night before fishing, and all through the lake
Not a creature was stirring, not even a snake;
The poles were stuck in the rod holders with care,
In hopes that a big fish would soon be there;
The kids were nestled all snug in the vessel,
While dreaming of fishes they soon would wrestle;
And mamma in her winter duds and I in my fishing hat,
Had just settled down on our watery mat,
When out on the lake there arose such a clatter,
I sprang to my feet to see what was the matter.
I flew to the stern where I saw a big splash, and
Before I knew it, I heard a big crash.
The moon on the breast of the water below
Gave a luster of silver and made everything glow,
When what to my wondering eyes should appear,
But a miniature boat pulled by eight tiny fish, or were they reindeer?
With a tall old driver, so lively and quick,
I knew in a moment it must be a trick.
More rapid than bonefish his coursers they came,
And he tooted and shouted, and called them by name;
"Now, Bass! Now, Trout! Now, Bream and Flathead, too!
On, Striper! On Perch! On Crappie and Blue!
To the top of the dam! To the head of the falls!
Now swim away! Swim away! Swim away all!"
As waves that before the wild hurricane fly,
When they meet with an obstacle, mount to the sky,
So up to our vessel the coursers they flew,
With a boat load of fish and Captain Gus, too.
And then, in a twinkling, I heard with a swish
The flipping and flopping of each little fish.
As I drew in my hand, and was turning around,
Down the mast came Captain Gus with a bound.
He was dressed in Red Gore-Tex, from his head to his toe,
And his clothes were all smelly from scales and minnows;

A box full of tackle he carried on his back,
And he looked like a fish peddler just opening his pack.
His eyes—they looked fishy! His dimples how merry!
His cheeks were like redfish, his nose like a cherry!
His droll little mouth was bowed like a rod,
And the beard on his chin was as white as a cod (fish).
The end of a fishing line he held tight in his teeth,
And the smoke from the motor encircled his head like a wreath;
He had a narrow face and a flat little belly,
It didn't shake much like a bowl full of jelly.
He wasn't chubby and plump, just a tall old elf,
That made me laugh when I saw him, in spite of myself;
A fishing rod in hand and a twist of his head,
Soon gave me to know I had nothing to dread;
He spoke not a word, but went straight to his work,
And filled all the stringers; then turned with a jerk,
And laying his finger aside of his nose,
And giving a nod, up the mast he rose;
He jumped in his boat, to his team gave a whistle,
And away they all swam with the speed of a missile.
But I heard him exclaim ere he drove out of sight,
"Good Fishing to all, and to all a good-night."

978-0-595-43348-3
0-595-43348-0

Printed in the United States
92684LV00005B/643-738/A